Linden, Madelaine
Gill.

Under the blanket

877227

DATE		

© THE BAKER & TAYLOR CO.

Under the Blanket

Under the Blanket

written and illustrated by
Madelaine Gill Linden

Little, Brown & Company
Boston Toronto

Also illustrated by Madelaine Gill Linden:

All Small by David McCord
Hortense by Jan Paul
Bunny Rabbit Rebus by David Adler

First Edition

Library of Congress Cataloging-in-Publication Data
Linden, Madelaine Gill.
   Under the blanket.
   Summary: Mouse, Bear, and Lion search the house from top to
bottom, looking everywhere for the missing Gillian.
   [1. Stories in rhyme] I. Title.
PZ8.3.L615Un 1987   [E]   86-14610
ISBN 0-316-52626-6

WOR

*Published simultaneously in Canada
by Little, Brown & Company (Canada) Limited*

Printed in the United States of America

For my mother and father

Two little creatures live in this house —
One is a lion and one is a mouse.

In this house lives Gillian, too.
A little girl whose shoes are blue.

She sits down with Lion and Mouse just at three
To share a green apple, some cookies, and tea.

Later they dress up in bracelets and rings,
Scarves, hats with feathers, and other fine things!

They draw with crayons, they build with blocks,
And make designs with pebbles and rocks.

Their friend Honey Bear sometimes joins them to play
And stays at the house till the end of the day.

Then Gillian gives Mouse and Lion a hug
And sings them to sleep on the yellow hearth rug.

But one afternoon when the clock had struck three
Gillian was not at the table for tea.

"She must be hiding!"
Mouse said in a burst.

"Under the bed is where we'll look first!"

And away they dashed past a green apple core,
And past a pink blanket that lay on the floor.

To the edge of the bed they ran in a flash
When Mouse tripped on the rug and fell with a crash.

"Oh, please don't cry, Mousie," the kind Lion said,
"You've only a very small bump on your head!"

Mouse wiped from each eye a single large tear.
"I'm fine!" she said bravely. "But Gillian's not here!"

So, on to the closet, along the far wall
They ran and they rummaged, stopping only to call:

"Where are you hiding? Oh, where can you be?
Have you forgotten it's time for our tea?"

Hearing no answer, they sped to the chest,
Where they found satin ribbons and an old robin's nest.

They searched in the shadow in back of the door,

And then in the basket of toys on the floor.

In back of the curtains, in back of the couch,

Close to the wall where someone might crouch.

From under the cushions they heard a voice shout,
"Help me! I'm stuck here! Please pull me out!"

They pulled and they tugged, and who should be there?
Oh, no, it's not Gillian, but their old friend Bear!

"I was chasing a ball that went faster than me!"
Bear said brightly, "And now I am ready for tea!"

"It's no time for eating!" Mouse said to Bear.
"Gillian is hiding; we can't find out where."

"Follow me," said Bear. "I will look for her, too.
"Under the table I saw something blue."

"Gillian's blue shoe!" Mouse exclaimed with delight.
"But Gillian," sighed Lion, "is nowhere in sight."

So, wondering where they should look for her next,
Mouse, Lion, and Bear all sat down perplexed.

How quiet the room was,
How still it was there!
Could Gillian have vanished into thin air?

Then without warning they heard a strange sound
And holding their breath the three looked around.

They couldn't believe it!

A thing so surprising!

They saw that the blanket was suddenly rising!

From under a corner there peeked a blue shoe,
Then up popped Gillian. "I've been waiting for you!

"I'm under the blanket—

Right here! Can't you see?

Why not come under the blanket with me?"

Now, where are Lion and Bear and Mouse?
They all must be hiding somewhere in this house!